# THE SandWitch

## A HALLOWEEN FABLE

WRITTEN BY JIM SCHISGALL
ILLUSTRATED BY JOHN TIMMINS
PRODUCTION DESIGN BY MICHAEL FERRARI

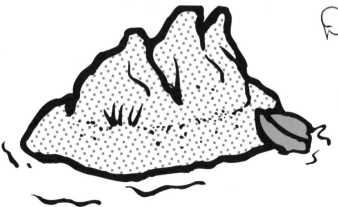

2016
Dear Mohammed,
Hope you have
a wonderful
Halloween!
Mrs. Simonian

Printed in the United States of America.

Library of Congress Catalog Card Number: 97-73688
ISBN: 1-890997-00-5

First Edition

**To My Daughter Alexandra**
*We all soar on the broomstick of her imagination.*

The Witch lived all alone on Sand Island with only the crabby Sand Crab and nosy Sand Piper to keep her company.

That was why she called herself the Sand Witch.

On a stormy Halloween night many years ago, lightning split her broomstick in two as she flew high above the ocean.

Now it was Halloween Eve again and the Sand Witch hoped for any way in which to escape.

Suddenly, a small sailboat washed ashore. A little girl was in its bow.

"Who are you?" the Sand Witch asked.

"I'm Alexandra," the girl replied. She was only eight years old.

"And what brings you here?" the Sand Witch asked.

Alexandra tried to remember what had happened. There was a sailboat ... a sudden storm ... an awesome wave ... but the rest was a blank. "I was sailing," she replied. "I must have fallen asleep. When I woke up, I found myself here."

"This is MY island and I say you must leave!" the Sand Witch warned.

"But I'm hungry and tired," Alexandra pleaded.

"And I'm angry because I can't fly away from here," the Witch replied.

"Why can't you fly?" Alexandra asked.

"Because my broomstick is broken," the Sand Witch sighed.

Alexandra was frightened. Would she ever see her home again? She looked inside her sailboat. And then she had an idea. "If I make you a new broomstick, will you feed me and fly me home?"

"And if I were to say 'yes'," the Sand Witch asked, "how would you make me a new broomstick when there's nothing here but sand and seaweed?"

"I'm smarter than you think," Alexandra answered.

"Go ahead, then," the Sand Witch commanded. "Make it!"

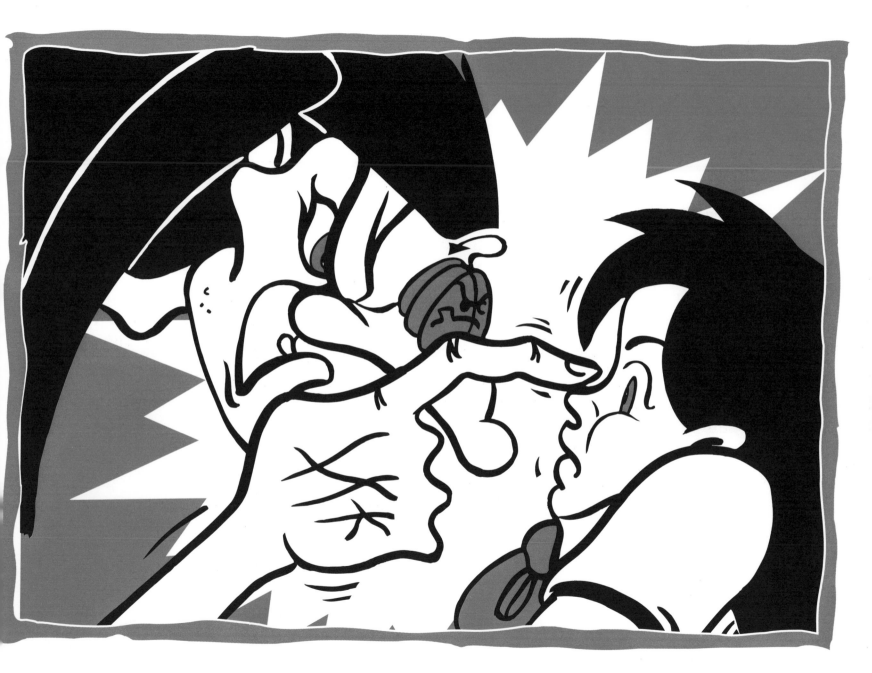

"**F**irst," Alexandra insisted, "you've got to promise to feed me and take me home."

The Sand Witch nodded, but her wrinkled fingers were crossed behind her back.

Alexandra returned to her sailboat and removed its mast. She took some seaweed that had washed ashore and tied it to the end of the mast. Home is not far away, she thought. As long as I can make this mast into a broomstick ...

The Sand Witch returned with a handful of dirty sand packed inside dried-out lily pads. "Here's your food!"

"What's that?" Alexandra asked, pinching her nose to avoid the terrible smell.

"A sandwich," the Sand Witch answered. There were worms and ants crawling everywhere and the sand was wet and sticky.

"No, thank you," Alexandra replied. "I think I'll eat when I get home!"

"That broomstick looks ready to fly," the Sand Witch said as she grabbed the mast. The Witch rubbed the bundled seaweed up-and-down.

Suddenly, the Sand Witch and her new broomstick began to **rise above** the sandy dunes.

"Don't forget me," Alexandra shouted. "Remember your promise!"

"HA, HA!" the Sand Witch replied as she flew in circles above Alexandra. "I had my fingers crossed behind my back when I made that promise!"

Alexandra's mouth dropped open.

"**Y**ou won't get far without this sail," Alexandra quickly warned, taking the sail from the sailboat. "If the wind blows hard, that broomstick will break and you'll tumble head first back into the sea."

Once before the Sand Witch's broomstick had broken while in flight. Could it happen again? Was the little girl telling the truth? "Why should I believe you?" the Sand Witch asked.

"Because we have to believe in each other if either of us is to escape from here," Alexandra observed. "I believed you when you promised to take me home. So you better believe me when I say you won't get far without this sail."

The little girl may have a point, the Sand Witch thought. "Climb aboard," she said. "Right behind me. And hold onto my waist."

Alexandra breathed deeply. Her plan had worked. But she didn't like holding the Sand Witch's waist. There was no body inside! Just an old faded cloth to hold onto.

Seconds later, the Sand Witch and Alexandra were flying into the Halloween sky, the crabby Sand Crab and nosy Sand Piper in tow.

Skeletons appeared from behind the clouds. Some grabbed at Alexandra.

"Why are these monsters attacking me?" she shouted.

"Because you're not one of us!" the Sand Witch answered.

Ghosts with spooky faces raced across the sky. The Sand Witch steered her broomstick away from all attackers. "Don't worry, little girl," she promised. "You're safe with me - as long as you hold onto that sail."

"Let's put the sail on before the broomstick breaks," Alexandra warned. "It feels like we're in a hurricane!"

Alexandra opened the sail and attached it to the broomstick.

Now, Alexandra took full command of the flight. She flew the broomstick as if she were its captain.

"This is fantastic!" the Sand Witch shouted. "I've never flown so fast."

Alexandra steered the broomstick away from all the dangerous monsters. Finally, her escape - her safety - was in her own hands.

Goblins flew by, their three arms waving in the winds. Vampires joined the chase. But Alexandra was more than their equal. She was, truly, the master of the Halloween skies!

"I've never seen a better pilot," the Sand Witch admitted.

Suddenly, through the clouds below, Alexandra spotted a very familiar home.

"Hold on tight," Alexandra warned. "We're heading in a new direction."

"Oh, please don't crash," the Sand Witch pleaded as the broomstick dove toward the ground below. "I couldn't bear another broken broomstick."

"Don't worry," Alexandra reassured her. "I want to get home safely, too."

Seconds later, the broomstick landed on Alexandra's bedroom window sill. "That was some fancy landing," the Witch observed. "You can be my captain anytime!"

**A**lexandra sighed as she wiggled herself through her open bedroom window.

"Where will you go from here? "Alexandra asked.

"To light Halloween pumpkins, of course," the Sand Witch replied. "What do you think this flaming wart is for?" she added, pointing to the pumpkin-wart in the middle of her crooked nose.

Wow, Alexandra thought. So that's why pumpkins are lit on Halloween! "And after tonight?" Alexandra asked.

"Back to Sand Island, I guess," the Sand Witch said in all honesty. "Who else will look after this crabby Sand Crab and nosy Sand Piper?"

"Watch out for strong winds," Alexandra warned. "You don't want another broken broomstick!"

As the Sand Witch flew back into the Halloween skies, the crabby Sand Crab and nosy Sand Piper waved good-bye. And Alexandra fell exhausted onto her very own and welcoming bed.

"Get up, get up!" her mother's voice interrupted. "You've been napping long enough. If you sleep any longer, you'll miss trick-or-treat."

Alexandra shook her head. "You must have had a terrible dream," her mother added. "You've been tossing and turning all afternoon."

Alexandra could hardly believe her ears. Had there been no Sand Witch? Had her flight been only a dream?

"Get yourself dressed before it turns dark outside," her mother ordered.

Alexandra put on her witch's costume as she tried to shake away her dream.

"I know you must be starved," her mother added. "So I prepared your favorite snack. A peanut butter and jelly sandwich."

"A *sandwich!*" Alexandra exploded. *"I'll never eat another sandwich in all my life!"*

THE

# END

# THE
# SandWitch
## A HALLOWEEN FABLE

Jim Schisgall, author, is a 63-year-old father of three pre-teen children. With this sensitive and engrossing story, he touches the heart of every child who has ever been fascinated by Halloween. The son of one of America's leading short-short story writers, Jim's extraordinary story-telling talents are revealed in this positive story about a child who builds her own strong character when she overcomes adversity. **The Sand Witch** is truly a story for the ages and one whose surprise ending will thrill children of all ages. Jim lives with his wife Beth and their three children in Syosset, New York.

John Timmins, illustrator, reveals a novel and captivating creativity in this, his first illustrated children's book. He captures both the spirit and mystique of Halloween with a wry sense of humor guaranteed to appeal to all children. John lives in Huntington, New York.